This book belongs to

_____

_____

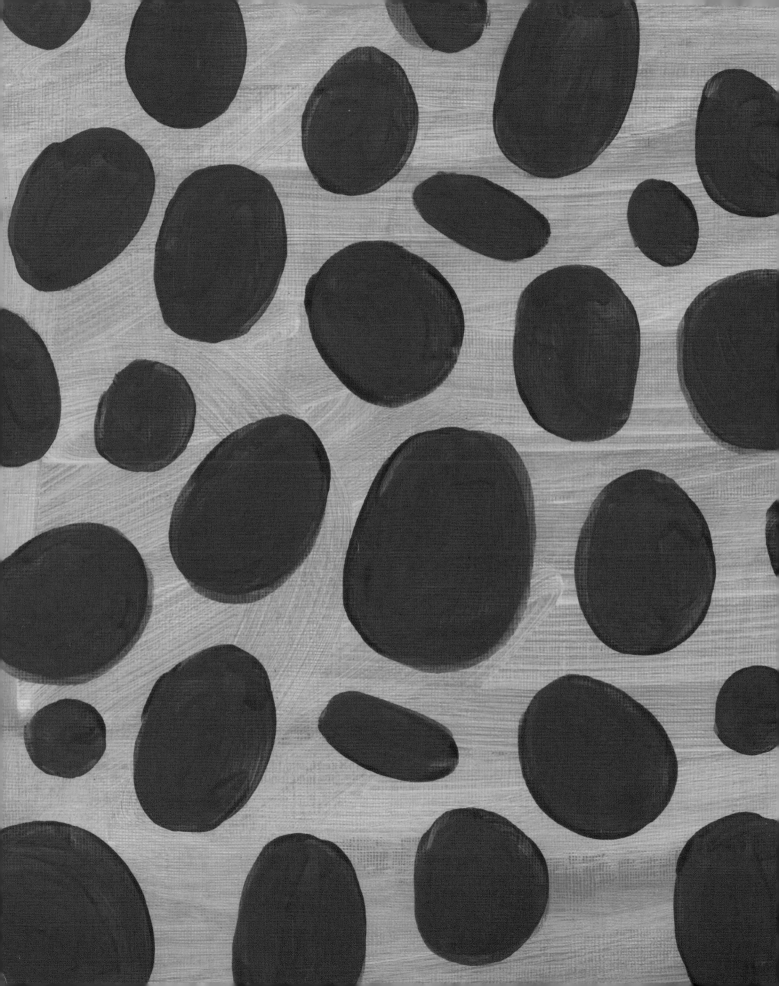

For Milla and Zac
C.V.

First published in Great Britain in 2012 by
Gullane Children's Books
185 Fleet Street, London, EC4A 2HS
www.gullanebooks.com

1 3 5 7 9 10 8 6 4 2

Text and illustrations © Catherine Väse 2012

ISBN: 978-1-86233-901-9

Printed and bound in China

The **BIG** HAIR Affair

Catherine
Vāse

GULLANE
CHILDREN'S BOOKS

Lawrence was the best hairdresser in the jungle.
He was a whizz with the scissors and a pro with the comb.
He snipped and shaped, sculpted and styled,
and even told his customers very funny jokes.

Lawrence could make anyone feel a million dollars.
Everyone loved him . . .

except Marvin.

Marvin just couldn't understand why Lawrence was so popular . . .

so he sneered,

he jeered,

and he did everything he could think of to make Lawrence look silly.

But things didn't always go to plan.

Then one day a letter
arrived for Lawrence:

Dear Lawrence,
As you know I am a HUGE
star and I have the most
STUNNING SPOTS in the
jungle. Everyone thinks
you're grrr-reat, so I
would love YOU to be
MY hairdresser!
See you tomorrow.
Yours famously,
Sonja X

"WOW!" cried Lawrence.

"Typical," tutted Marvin. "Everyone loves Lawrence."
But he had a plan to make Lawrence look very silly indeed...

That night Marvin found Lawrence's special hair dye.
The label said: FOR STUNNING SPOTS.

Then he did something
VERY naughty!

Lawrence's big day arrived,
and so did his special customer!
"Step this way, Sonja," said Lawrence proudly.

Carefully he began to snip and shape,
sculpt and style . . .

whilst telling his very best jokes. He then applied a generous dollop of his special hair dye for

STUNNING SPOTS.

Finally the big moment arrived. "Sonja," said Lawrence, "what do you think of your stunning new . . .

Sonja gave Lawrence
an extra long hug,
and off she went to do
her famous thing.

Marvin's plan had failed spectacularly.
"Everyone loves Lawrence even more," he howled,
"and no one in the whole wide world...

"loves ME!"

Marvin felt very, very alone.

But just then
he heard a voice.
"Hello, Marvin.
You look like you need a friend!"

It was Lawrence!

For the first time ever, Marvin couldn't find anything mean to say.

"Hello, Lawrence," he mumbled, and then...

. . . out tumbled everything.

How he'd sneered and jeered,
how he'd tried to make Lawrence look silly
and, finally, how he tried to ruin Sonja's hair.

"I'm sorry, Lawrence!" he cried.

"Your trick was very naughty," said Lawrence.
"But I forgive you. Let's be friends!"

And he had an idea . . .

"Your stripes gave Sonja's hair something extra-special.
Why don't you come and work with me.
We'll make a Marv-ellous team!"

And they did.

"Do you like your new haircut, Marvin?"
said Lawrence.
"It's grrrr-eat!" said Marvin. "Just like you!
Care for a cup of tea, Lawrence?"

Other books for you to enjoy...

I Love You Mummy...I Love You Daddy!
Catherine Väse

If Mummy were a sound, what would she be?
The gentle purr of a cat!

But what would Mummy be if she were a place, a fruit or a bird?
Find out then flip the book over to see what Daddy would be
if he were a toy, a meal or a noise!

"A delightful celebration of love" MUMSENSE

Trixie Ten
Sarah Massini

Trixie Ten has NINE brothers and sisters. Nine NOISY brothers and
sisters. How she longs for some quiet and some space of her own!
So one day she sets off alone to find it.
NO noisy brothers and sisters...
It will be perfect... Won't it?!

Twinkle, Twinkle, Little Star
Jane Cabrera

Twinkle, twinkle, little star, how I wonder what you are...

In the dry desert and the wet jungle, in the sleeping city
and the icy Pole, join baby animals and their parents
as they share the wonder of a twinkling star!

Dog in Boots
Greg Gormley • illustrated by **Roberta Angaramo**

Puss in Boots has splendid boots – and Dog wants some too!
But will Dog's new boots be right for digging and scratching
and swimming...and all the things he loves to do?

"Children will laugh out loud"
KIRKUS REVIEWS (Starred Review)

"Dog's smile will capture readers' hearts"
SCHOOL LIBRARY JOURNAL (Starred Review)